MAYHEM
IN THE
MOONGARDEN

© 2021 Mayhem in the Moongarden by E. L. Seer. All Rights Reserved. Published by The Ridge Publishing Group. ETHAN FOX, ETHAN FOX BOOKS, the BOOK LOGO, KIDSSTAGRAMCLUB, CARETAKER WORLD, KIDSSTAGRAM LOGO, and all related characters and elements, names and related indicia are trademarks and/or registered trademarks of The Ridge Publishing Group.

RidgePublishingGroup.com
EthanFoxBooks.com
KidsStagram.com

Library of Congress Cataloging-in-Publication Data is available upon request.
ISBN 978-1-884573-93-4 (e-book)
ISBN 978 1-884573-94-1 (paperback)
ISBN 978-1-884573-95-8 (hardcover)

Cover illustrated by Connie Lin
Interior illustrated by Nancy Batra

Printed in the United States of America

Mayhem
in the
Moongarden

By E. L. Seer
Cover illustrated by Connie Lin
Interior illustrated by Nancy Batra

Ethan Fox Books
an imprint of The Ridge Publishing Group
Coeur d'Alene, Idaho, U.S.A

MEET THE

Grubner Trowel
Mrs. Moongarden's
right hand man.

Ravisher
Pesky gluttonous
creatures that infest
any food source.

Mildred Moongarden
Caretaker head botanist and
creator of the Moongarden.

Hayley Ravenwood
Daughter of the
Caretaker Headmistress.

Irvin McGillicutty
Butler and keeper of
The Residence.

CHARACTERS

Gruggins McGhee
Grumpling of the house
at The Residence.

Wordly Pagemore
Bookworm and keeper of the
Caretaker Arts & Literature archive.

Albert
Red pyrodevlin from
Hades: the 'R' in RGB.

Linus
Green pyrodevlin from
Ceres: the 'G' in RGB.

Newton
Bluepyrodevlin from
Atlantis: the 'B' in RGB.

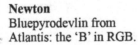

Prologue

THE CARETAKER UNIVERSE

Our story takes place in a mysterious world within our own—a world where the Caretakers watch over the human race and protect it from evil. The Caretakers are a coalition of intelligent beings from the four elemental worlds: Atlantis, Ceres, Hades, and Zephyr. Caretakers inhabit The Residence, their home base on Earth hidden and unknown to the humans they protect.

The Moongarden is a special place within The Residence created by Mildred Moongarden.

Wonderous and otherworldly plant-life inhabit the Moongarden proper, while its special purpose Moon Orchard provides the Caretakers with all of their food needs on earth.

Grubner Trowel's greatest desire is to gain more responsibility and earn the respect of his mentor, Mildred Moongarden. Eager to please, Grubner gets his chance when Mildred is called away on important business and asks him to look after her prized Moongarden. But when Ravishers suddenly infest the Moongarden and its all-important orchard, mayhem ensues.

Grubner rushes to save the Caretaker's primary food source, the Moongarden's Moon Orchard. He quickly learns that earthly Ravishers are intelligent creatures, and he has his hands full in his battle to exterminate them. Will Grubner prevail against the witty pests before they wreak total devastation? Or will Mildred return beforehand and find "Mayhem in the Moongarden?"

Chapter 1

WEDDING PLANS

The fresh scent of morning dew tickled Grubner's nose as he breathed the fresh morning air in the Moongarden. Today is going to be a wonderful day, he thought to himself. He glanced down to re-read the urgent message from Mrs. Moongarden. It read:

"Dear Grubner, I hope this letter finds your spirits flowering with bliss. I've been called away on crucial matters, and my wits are as frayed as a feathering whistle vine in a rainbow storm. It is with utmost urgency I ask for your assistance. Please meet me in the clearing as soon as the sun sprouts. We must harvest a blossoming plan for the upcoming weeks. Kind regards, Old Moonshoes."

Old Moonshoes was a nickname Mrs. Moongarden had given herself, and in true 'Moonshoes' fashion, the letter sounded as whacky as its author. By the time he finished reading, Grubner still had no idea what she had asked of him.

Grubner Trowel was a three-foot-tall dwarf with big blue eyes, white hair, a Santa's beard, and a kind smile. He wore a green cloth garment draped over his body like a bedsheet. It hung above his brown high-topped boots, and a black belt secured it below his potbelly.

Grubner, the fourth of seven Trowel brothers from his mother's first and only earth-born litter, hated being the middle sibling. Being one of seven dwarfs led to a lot of ribbing by other Caretaker kids at The Residence. He and his brothers had heard every Snow White comment ever invented while growing up. But Grubner didn't mind because he enjoyed the old Disney classic.

"Hi-Ho, Hi-Ho, it's off to work I go," Grubner sang out loud as he skipped down the path to meet up with Mrs. Moongarden.

Grubner approached a thatch of shrubbery with brilliantly colored flowers, like butterflies, their wings opened and closed as if ready to take flight. Mrs. Moongarden's head popped up from behind the tall bushes.

"Lisa's flowers will flutter away soon," Mrs. Moongarden said. "I find it pleasing when they fly off to make little shrubs of their own, brings a tear to my eye every time."

Mrs. Moongarden named all of her creations, and Lisa was the name of the Butterfly Shrub. Mildred Moongarden's sweet grandmotherly demeanor

11

made her a favorite of everyone. Her wrinkled rosy cheeks always cradled a smile beneath the round glasses perched on her nose. She wore a blue and white sundress on her slightly plump frame and a floral bonnet over her frail white hair.

"Simply tickled pink I am, you are showing up so early. Come, we've no time to waste. Rosebud is expecting us. I will explain on the way."

He followed Mrs. Moongarden down a different path leading deeper into the Moongarden to the right. Grubner was Mildred's 'little helper' around the Moongarden and was thrilled and excited to have been summoned by her for something sounding so important.

"Percy the pear tree has asked for the branch of Alicia the apple tree," Mrs. Moongarden said, "and she said yes! The wedding will take place in the clearing near the Moon Orchard in two weeks. We've barely enough time to plan."

Mrs. Moongarden let out a deep sigh.

"And to make matters worse, I've been called away on important business. A Skyclimber seedling has made its way into the human world. It is only a matter of time before she reaches the clouds and humans discover her."

Mrs. Moongarden stopped at a small bush with a mixture of blue and red leaves.

Several small twigs poked up and away from within the thicket and curled into the shape of a pig's tail. A thin, stringy vine hung to the ground at the end of each pigtail, and bright purple berries slowly slid down like on a guidewire. Small red cones beneath the end of each vine collected the berries.

"I'm afraid we may need to harvest all of Linnie's dwindle-berries to contain the growing Skyclimber. We must move her to safety. The human world is no place for a young Skyclimber."

Linnie was Mrs. Moongarden's pet name for the Itsy Bitzy bush, another of her ingenious creations. Each Itsy Bitzy grew up to ten dwindle-berries a day on every one of its pigtails. The fruit was highly valued due to its ability to shrink things, even people. One dwindle-berry will cause the near-halving of the consuming party, but the shrinkage is reversible by simply eating an equal number of shrunken dwindle-berries.

"Grubner will gather a sack full of dwindle-berries for Moonshoes."

"I once witnessed a gluttonous-gordgerat eat two dozen," Mrs. Moongarden said. "Poor creature disappeared from existence, didn't save any berries for a return to size."

"One must plan ahead when eating dwindle-berries," Grubner said.

"Oh my, we mustn't get distracted from our purpose," she said as she started back down the path at a frantic pace, and Grubner trailed behind.

When they arrived at the clearing, Rosebud stood by a fold-out table beneath the shade of Alicia the apple tree. A pile of invitations sat in front of her as she folded them in half and addressed them. As soon as she set one down, the invite would fold itself into a paper airplane and take off for delivery.

Rosebud dressed like Mrs. Moongarden, bonnet, and all. Mini-Moonshoes, some called her, but Rosebud's youth made her look more like Mildred's granddaughter. Her flowing strawberry blonde hair, bright green eyes, and matching green lipstick gave her an odd but beautiful appeal.

"Good morning," said Rosebud.

"I trust all is going smoothly, and you have accounted for all of the invitees?" Mrs. Moongarden asked.

"Smooth as a silk-flower."

"Terrific, our plans have blossomed."

A confused frown swept across Grubner's face. Why did she summon him with such urgency if Rosebud and Moonshoes already had everything planned?

"Okay," he said as the color drained from his face. "If there will be nothing else, Grubner will fetch dwindle-berries for Moonshoes."

"Oh my, I am sorry," Mrs. Moongarden replied. "My old noggin isn't as snappy as it used to be. Please forgive me for getting sidetracked. I have asked you here for an urgent reason."

Grubner perked up as the corners of his smile nearly reached the edges of his eyes.

"I must ask you for a significant favor. I must ask you to tend to the Moongarden while I am gone."

Grubner's forehead crinkled to make room for his eyes widening like saucers.

"Rosebud has offered to help, but she is far too busy planning Alicia and Percy's wedding. I have tremendous faith in Grubner, but if the responsibility is too much for you—"

"Grubner accepts. Grubner will take care of the Moongarden for Moonshoes."

"Whip-dilly doodles," Mrs. Moongarden said. "I'm as pleased as a peach. If you need any help, Rosebud will be available in case of an emergency. Now, I have provided Irvin with several days worth of supplies. But he will be stopping by to discuss his needs so you can properly plan the Moon Orchard's crop configuration."

Irvin McGillicutty was the keeper of The Residence and the right-hand man to the Caretaker Headmistress. He performed all manner of duties around The Residence, including procuring the food required to cook for an army of hungry Caretakers. And the Moon Orchard played an essential role as it supplied Irvin with all of his daily needs at The Residence.

Grubner got his final marching orders from Moonshoes. Afterward, he hung around and listened to her and Rosebud blabber on about wedding plans.

Grubner had worked as Mildred Moongarden's assistant for years and had learned a lot from her. He regarded Old Moonshoes as his mentor and even carried a copy of her book 'Moonshoes Guide to the Moongarden' in his pocket. It was all he had ever wanted, to be accepted by her and given more responsibility. Today was a wonderful day, and Grubner's dreams were coming true.

Chapter 2

GRUBNER'S TROUBLES

Grubner's eyes squinted nearly shut as he gazed up at the enormous vine stretching into the pillowy white clouds in the sky. The Skyclimber is indeed a marvel to behold, he thought. How on earth is Mrs. Moongarden going to corral a young one growing in the wild? He had no idea, but today began his chance to prove himself more than a trusted helper. The Moongarden would flourish during Mildred's absence, and Grubner would handle everything himself without Rosebud's help.

For his first rounds of the day, Grubner decided to walk every single path through the Moongarden and take notes on anything requiring his attention. Thus far, things didn't look so good, and Grubner's notepad already brimmed with writing. He found a lot of things out of place or ever so slightly disturbed. Mrs. Moongarden would never leave things in such an unkempt state. Grubner's stomach churned with angst, something strange was going on, but he had no idea what.

As he walked past the burning Firelyte Shrub, a twinkle of light tickled the corner of his eye as its flames flickered. But when he turned to glance at the blazing bush, the encompassing inferno appeared normal.

"Now I'm seeing things," he said, "and talking to myself."

Grubner continued along the path, and something disturbing grabbed his attention. Wendy, the Withering Froo, was all balled up in her protective shielding leaves, or "shleaves" as Moonshoes called them. A boulder of tree bark stood where a beautiful giant red flower usually sat. Something must have disturbed it for that to happen, but he found no apparent culprit when he scanned the area.

Grubner made his way to the clearing where he had met Moonshoes and Rosebud the previous day. He and Irvin were scheduled to meet at the Moon Orchard to discuss Irvin's supply needs for the following days. The Moon Orchard was another of Mrs. Moongarden's ingenious creations, a massive garden created to supply all of the Caretaker's daily food requirements at The Residence. It was designed in sections, each of which could be reconfigured on a rotating basis to supply Irvin with his ever-changing daily needs.

When he arrived, he stopped in horror. Row upon row of uprooted and devoured vegetation lay spread across the expansive garden. Something foul was afoot in the Moon Orchard. Grubner walked to the remains of a nearby peacock plant where tattered feathers lay scattered, the buttery core gnawed to a nub. Nearly one-quarter of the Moon Orchard had been consumed, and only stems, leaves, roots, and bulbs remained.

"Schnickyrooners and things like that," Irvin ranted as he approached from behind. "Hotdog worms eat green dirt noodles on the side of the flying turtle lips. And when they scream loud enough, the pig warts won't even make a sound like they did before brunch."

"Stop it, Irvin! I have no time for your jibber-jabber. Something terrible has happened; someone sabotaged the Moon Orchard."

"Oh my, what happened to the Moon Orchard?" Irvin asked as he snapped out of his rant.

Irvin McGillicutty was tall with white skin resembling candle wax, and his face had little definition. He wore a black tuxedo with a bow tie and a rose corsage. Irvin worked as the butler, chef, maid, and handyman of The Residence, you name it, and he probably had a hand in it.

"Don't worry," Irvin said, "I'll go fetch Rosebud. She'll know what to do."

"You will do no such thing! The Moongarden is under my watch, and I will take care of this."

"Sure you will. That's why your face looks like this." Irvin's face morphed into a funny version of Grubner's face. His mouth drooped ridiculously wide open, down to his neckline, and his eyes covered half his face and turned as round as tennis balls.

"I have everything under control," Grubner insisted. "If you say so," Irvin replied as his face returned to its usual department store dummy appearance. "In the meantime, I have no current need for supplies. Old Moonshoes made sure I stocked up before she left."

"She did?" Grubner asked as a slight frown invaded his face.

"Must have foreseen Grubner's troubles," Irvin said.

Grubner spent the next five minutes smoothing things over with Irvin and convincing him not to tell Rosebud what had happened. Finally, Irvin reluctantly agreed and gave Grubner a list of his future needs. He would return in a day or two to check on the status of his next order.

Once Irvin left, Grubner wasted no time cleaning up the trashed areas so he could replant the damaged section of the Moon Orchard as fast as possible.

"Did Mrs. Moongarden foresee troubles for Grubner?" he thought to himself. If so, it meant she didn't have any faith in him and only chose him because Rosebud was too busy. Either way, Grubner would prove himself capable to them all.

Chapter 3

THE RAVISHERS

Grubner continued cleaning up the mess in the Moon Orchard the following day. Rosebud stopped by on her way to visit Alicia and Percy to discuss their ceremony and reception details.

"Howdy-doody Grubner, is everything running smoothly?" she asked. "I thought I would stop by and see how things are going."

"Smooth as a silk-flower," Grubner said with a wink and a smile. "I'm nearly ready for the next reconfigure."

Luckily, he cleared enough of the mess away, so Rosebud didn't notice anything out of the ordinary.

"You're doing a wonderful job. Anyway, I must run along. The wedding is not going to plan itself, toodle-oo."

He spent the next few hours looking over his shoulder as he cleaned up the rest of the Moon Orchard. Could Mrs. Moongarden have asked Rosebud to spy on him? Surely not. She wasn't that kind of person. Still, he would be prepared, just in case.

"Grubner will show them all," he said to himself as he scooped up the last few remnants of consumed plant remains.

Grubner stretched his arms out and yawned, then sat down on the grass to lean against a tree stump at the edge of the Moon Orchard. He tossed a rock into the nearby pond and stared at the circular ripples as they grew across its surface.

"I hear there are troublemakers in your midst," a voice said from over Grubner's shoulder.

Grubner turned his head to see who spoke to him. His old friend, Gruggins McGhee, stood behind him on the stump. Gruggins was a bluish-green mouse-sized creature called a grumpling. He had the face of an old man with a fat bulbous nose, tall blue Tweetie-bird eyes, and two moth-like wings with a purple and yellow eye pattern.

"Hey Gruggins, I bet I can guess where you heard that on my first try."

"Of course, you can. Irvin has been blabbing all over The Residence. That mush-mouthed-morph-dork never keeps his trap shut."

Grubner and Gruggins were friends, so he decided to confide in him.

"I don't know what to do, Gruggins. I don't know what happened, and now I'm ready to replant the damaged section of the Moon Orchard. It may happen again, and I am freaking out."

"Which is why I dropped by," Gruggins said. "Maybe I can aid you in exposing the culprit, and together we will get to the bottom of this."

"Thank you, Gruggins. I would like your help, my dear friend."

"Sit tight while I take a glide around to investigate." Gruggins fluttered off to search the area from above for signs of Grubner's troubles.

Gruggins would take time to flutter around the expansive Moon Orchard. So, in the meantime, Grubner would use his break time wisely. He pulled out his elemental modulator. A small iPhone-like device referred to as an ELMO. Grubner tapped on the ELMO's screen, and a list with Irvin's order popped up. He studied the list but did not get very far because Gruggins returned and landed on the tree stump.

"Well? Did you find anything?" Grubner asked.

"I sure did."

"What did you find?"

"You've got an infestation, my friend. The garden is infested with Ravishers."

"Ravishers? What are Ravishers?" Grubner asked.

"They are nasty gluttonous creatures that eat almost anything. I'm surprised they didn't devour the whole Moon Orchard. Must be a small infestation, but you better eradicate them before they multiply, and Mildred returns to a Nonegarden."

Gruggins hopped onto Grubner's shoulder.

"Head that way, and I will show you the cause of your troubles," Gruggins said. He pointed towards an undisturbed portion of the Moon Orchard. "Behind the row of peacock-plants."

Grubner approached a tall line of colorful bushes resembling giant peacock feathers arranged in circular tiers around small hills. But they were not actually hills and consisted of mounds of peacock butter the limbs excreted as they grew. The feathers tickled Grubner's face as he slid between two of the plants, and Gruggins ducked to avoid getting knocked from his shoulder. They emerged into another small garden area where rows of carrots, radishes, and other vegetables lay ruined. Grubner's eyes widened, and his lips tightened into an angry smirk.

"Here we are," Gruggins said.

"But I don't see anything except for more devastation."

"Oh, I almost forgot, you can't see them, they cloak themselves, but I'll fix that."

Gruggins snapped his fingers, and the Ravishers slowly came into view. Grubner cringed at the sight of four black pumpkin-shaped creatures the size of basketballs. Their heads were almost nothing but a mouth full of dull chomping

32

teeth. Bright orange-yellow light emanated from their mouth, eyes, and line markings like a fire burning from within. Stubby little legs sat barely visible below their round bodies, while thick and lanky dark green arms dragged on the ground in front of them to scoop food into their faces.

At first, the Ravishers kept chomping away at the garden and ignored Grubner and Gruggins' presence. "They don't realize I have de-cloaked them," Gruggins whispered to Grubner. "What do you say we let them know?"

"Ahemmmm," Grubner cleared his throat loudly as he and Gruggins glared down at the creatures.

The Ravishers stopped all at once as their round bodies slowly pivoted upwards to point their eyes up at Grubner and Gruggins.

"Boo," Gruggins said.

The Ravisher's black eyes grew to the size of silver dollars, and their arms swiftly became long legs hoisting them off the ground and running away fast.

"Boo," Grubner repeated as the Ravishers ran for their lives like scared mice.

After scaring the Ravishers away, Gruggins hung around to give his buddy a pep talk. He warned Grubner the creatures would return and offered his assistance. Grubner thankfully declined but was grateful to his friend for exposing the culprits. Before leaving, Gruggins gave one final word of advice and showed his friend how to use his ELMO to adjust the Moongarden's light so the Ravishers could no longer cloak themselves. Grubner's task would be a whole lot easier if the Ravishers were not invisible when they ravished.

Chapter 4

SPLASH DOWN

Sweat droplets trickled down Grubner's cheeks, and his beard quickly soaked them up. The Ravishers had returned, so he raked up the remains of more wilted vegetation in the Moon Orchard. He had adjusted the Moongarden's light settings as Gruggins had suggested and made the morning rays more intense, but so far, he had not spotted any of the nasty creatures.

After cleaning up, he decided to explore every inch of the Moon Orchard to search for more damage. But he would not ignore the rest of the massive Moongarden, so he enlisted the help of his six brothers: Grabner, Gribner, Grobner, Gripner, Gropner, and Daryl. They assembled near the huge pond adjacent to the clearing and Moon Orchard.

Grubner gave them their marching orders, and they would report back with their findings.

"Sleepy and Sneezy, you two will take the Skyclimber area," Grubner said. "Grumpy and Bashful will take the courtyard and ruins, and that leaves the remainder of the Moongarden for Happy and Dopey."

Grubner's brothers hated when he made Snow White jokes, but they knew his ribbing was all in fun, and they would do anything for their brother Doc. It would not be so funny if the names didn't match their personalities so closely, Grubner thought; whoever wrote the story must have met his siblings.

While his brothers paired off and departed for the Moongarden proper, Grubner would concentrate on the Moon Orchard, where he knew more troubles would surface. So, he walked towards the Moon Orchard's center and stopped short of a tall barrier of foliage. Thorny black vines slithered out from beneath the wall of vegetation like serpents. They crept directly towards him and were nearly upon him when he pulled out his ELMO and tapped at its screen.

"A little too close for comfort," Grubner said, "but you Creeping Tanglers won't get me."

The thorny vines slowly retreated under the black wall as it unraveled into an archway for Grubner to walk through. The Creeping Tangler barrier wall was another of Mrs. Moongarden's wondrous creations, designed to trap any vermin infesting the Moon Orchard. But so far, the Ravishers had steered clear of the tanglers.

Grubner continued through the archway and realized he had never been this deep into the Moon Orchard. Finally, he came upon a row of six-foot-tall trees with thin straight trunks and big white globes of growth on top like giant dandelions. The balls on top formed from hundreds of foot-long twigs holding a perfect white egg at the end like skewers.

"The eggplants are untouched," Grubner said, "I thought for sure they would have ravished these by now."

Grubner continued his rounds and found nothing else out of place. Finally, he came to the hill at the back of the Moon Orchard where Mrs. Moongarden's prized Mimicking Melon trees grew. As he reached the top of the knoll, everything appeared to be in order. He stood at the foot of one of the tall trees and gazed up into its branches where hundreds of melon fruits the size of tennis balls were hanging. Tiny watermelons, cantaloupe, honeydew, and various other melon replicas hung, ripe and ready.

As he lowered his gaze, he focused down the row of forest and spotted one at the end that had fallen. His walk turned to a jog as he quickly approached the fallen timber.

"No, please no," he yelled, "not one of her prized melon trees."

Tears welled up in his eyes as he scanned the destruction. Bare branches and scattered leaves were all that remained of the beautiful Mimicking Melon. "I'll teach those horrid creatures," Grubner said as he ground his teeth. "They'll learn not to ravish Old Moonshoes' wonderful creations."

Grubner's brothers returned from their rounds and reported nothing out of the ordinary. So, after his discovery atop melon tree hill, he thought long and hard about how to react and came up with a plan to show the Ravishers who they were messing with. First, with the help of his brothers, he would climb one of the Mimicking Melon trees and hide in its branches. Then, when the Ravishers attacked it, he would pounce on them and scare them off. If he scared them bad enough, maybe they would not return.

Since the culprit always returned to the crime scene, Grubner picked out a tree right next to the fallen one near the edge of the hill. His six brothers got on their hands and knees and arranged themselves into a small staircase, three at the base, two on the next level, and one on the next. They reached barely high enough for Grubner to climb and grab the lowest branch to pull himself up.

Once safely in place, his brothers retreated to their homes for the day.

He hung out for nearly three hours, and with only two hours of light left in the day, all remained quiet. An hour later, Grubner's eyes grew heavy as he strained to keep them open. Ten minutes later, the sound of his snores filled the air.

Day faded to early evening when Grubner awoke to a grunting and gnawing noise. He peered down as his eyes came into focus on the sight of four

Ravishers below him chomping at the base of his tree. Ready to pounce, Grubner's tree abruptly angled sideways and fell swiftly. It hit hard at the edge of the hill and bounced, knocking Grubner out and sending him tumbling down the steep incline. He rolled to the bottom of the knoll and into the muddy end of the pond that wrapped around the backside of the Moon Orchard.

It took him several minutes to inch his way out of the thick deep muck. When he finally emerged from the goop, Grubner looked like a giant chocolate-covered dwarf. Mud oozed down his entire body as he glared up the hill. One of the Ravishers was standing at the edge of the hill, peering down at Grubner while the others continued to chomp away. This Ravisher was different than the others; the top of his head angled to a shallow cone just deep enough to hold the thick ring of thorns circling its head like a crown. The lead Ravisher continued to glare down as it let out a loud shrill laugh. Grubner's face felt flush as he raised his fists and yelled up at the Ravishers.

"This is not the last you pests have seen of Grubner Trowel. I will get all of you devils."

But the other Ravishers paid no attention to his rant and only stopped munching melons long enough to join their leader in laughter. By the time Grubner washed away the mud and hiked back up the hill, the Ravishers were gone, and another Mimicking Melon tree was destroyed.

Chapter 5

CORN RAVISHED

The clean odor of rain tickled Grubner's nose as he strolled on one of the Moongarden's many dirt pathways. But there wasn't a cloud in the sky, and it could only mean one thing – he would soon witness the dance of the Trembling Nomads. Grubner always got a kick out of their chaotic tango, so he hurried down the path to their enclosure.

"Well, at least the Moongarden is business as usual, and the infestation is confined to the Moon Orchard," Grubner thought to himself.

He stopped at the white picket fence surrounding tiny evergreen trees, their tops peaked forward like penguin heads. They resembled little people, each with two pine-covered arm branches and two brown leg trunks. Grubner watched closely as the nomads slowly raised their arm branches skyward and trembled violently like a group of little people shaking their fists at the sky.

Grubner's cheeks bunched into a smile as he anticipated what would happen. They would stop trembling any moment now, pop their trunks from the ground, and run around the pen bumping into one another like bumper cars. But instead, to his surprise, they popped up and formed a perfect row. Grubner had never seen this before, but Moonshoes had told him of it.

He gazed in astonishment as they joined branches, hopped up and down, and kicked their trunks around in unison like Irish dancers.

"Seedlings will be coming soon," he said. "Am I ever going to catch a break?"

Trembling Nomad infants were not hard to deal with, but it meant he would have to wrap their enclosure, or he would have seedlings roaming free in the Moongarden. And given his current struggles battling the pesky Ravishers, his to-do list grew longer by the day.

He continued on his way to the Moon Orchard where more destruction likely awaited his arrival. As he passed by Wendy the Withering Froo, Grubner stopped to examine one of Mrs. Moongarden's latest creations – a small shrub of Squid Blossoms. The pink flowers donned yellow and red spots resembling eyes. They had oblong bodies with long thin petals, like tentacles at the end. He bent down to sniff their sweet aromatic scent and could almost taste it. The delicate flowers grasped the end of his nose with their fragile tentacles. It tickled as he gently pulled away from their grasp and continued the journey, he dreaded to the Moon Orchard.

Grubner closed his eyes and crossed his fingers as he approached the Moon Orchard. Maybe the Ravishers had gotten their fill devouring two whole Mimicking Melon trees. Of course, he wasn't counting on it, but at least he'd hope for the best.

When he opened his eyes, the carnage was worse than he imagined. Husks and stalks littered the empty dirt field where the cornfield from his latest reconfigure should have stood. And to make matters worse, Irvin would be arriving soon to check on tomorrow's order. But Mrs. Moongarden had developed tools to deal with such emergencies. If he could clear out the devastation in a couple of hours and replant Irvin's cornfields, he would use some of Mildred's special Moongrow fertilizer to grow the crops overnight and still have plenty of time for the morning harvest. Grubner would need to call on his brothers for help once again.

"Shnickyrooners and schnackleboxes and things like that," Irvin's said in a goofy tone as he approached. "A giant fiddle-stick always disappoints its mother when the zoo is open for snail cookies. But you should never tell the sleeping lizard how to drive a finicky goober elf."

"Stop it, Irvin. I have far too many troubles as it is. Why are you always babbling?"

"Well, now, someone woke up on the wrong side of the tree-hut."

"I'm dealing with a nasty Ravisher infestation."

Irvin scanned the ravished cornfield and turned to face Grubner.

"Of course, Grubner's got everything under control. No problems at all, just as you promised.

Except for maybe over there—" he pointed at the cornfield. "And over there, and there, and there and right there." Arms morphed out from Irvin's body to point all around the destroyed pasture.

"Grubner will take care of this," he said as he let out a big sigh.

"What am I going to do for corn tomorrow?" Irvin asked. "I know . . . I will grow it out of my ears."

Irvin's four extra arms retreated into his body as two sizable ears of corn pushed their way out of the sides of his head and fell to the ground.

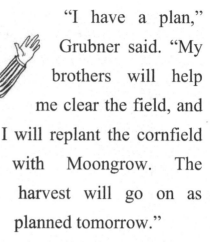

"I have a plan," Grubner said. "My brothers will help me clear the field, and I will replant the cornfield with Moongrow. The harvest will go on as planned tomorrow."

"If you say so."

"I just need to make sure those pests don't come back beforehand."

"You should build a scarecrow," Irvin suggested. "Humans use them all the time, and they never have Ravishers in their cornfields."

"Great idea, thank you," Grubner said. "If the humans can scare them away, Grubner will too."

"Happy to help, good luck, and see you soon." Irvin turned to leave but then turned back. "I almost forgot; Hayley Ravenwood will be joining the harvest tomorrow. The poor dear's been sad ever since Ethan Fox returned to the human world. She is in a funk."

"Ethan Fox," Grubner repeated.

"Indeed," Irvin said, "the hybrid child himself was in our midst. I do hope master Ethan is doing well, it has been nearly six months, and I have not heard a word about him."

"Well then," Grubner said, "we will try to cheer Miss Hayley up at the harvest."

After Irvin's exit, Grubner contacted his brothers on his ELMO. They arrived quickly, and in no time, had cleared away the rubble and replanted Irvin's cornfield. But it was only the beginning of Grubner's plan. Next, they would build a human-engineered totem to keep the Ravishers away. But first, they would travel to Market Square to buy supplies for the project.

The Moongarden grew dark by the time they finally made it back. There were barely enough Trowel siblings to carry all the supplies on Grubner's list. Nevertheless, the brothers were undeterred. They would build Grubner's masterpiece and fix the Ravishers for good.

Grubner and his helpers worked long into the night on the enormous monument. A silvery moon lit the night's sky and gave them enough light to admire their work.

"It would sure scare me if I were a Ravisher," Grubner said as he gazed up at his creation.

His brothers nodded in agreement.

Chapter 6

AN HONEST MISTAKE

Grubner waited at the entrance to the Moongarden when Irvin and Hayley arrived through the Hall of Doorways. He didn't return home until after midnight and hardly slept due to his excitement level. He also hadn't checked the Moon Orchard yet because there was no need. The Ravishers would be miles away by now, hiding from the masterpiece he and his brothers built to guard the cornfield.

"Good morning, Miss Hayley," he said. "May a dozen candied foxtails brighten your day." He knelt in front of Hayley and held up a bouquet of colorful treats.

"How thoughtful, Grubner," Hayley replied with a smile. "I love candied foxtails. Thank you."

Hayley was the daughter of the Caretaker Headmistress. She had golden blonde hair, blueish-green eyes, a petite nose, a rosy smile, and a charming demeanor.

Grubner turned to Irvin with fire in his eyes. "I have taken care of everything," he said. "We stayed up late last night working on it, and boy is it scary."

"Will your brothers be joining us for the harvest?" Irvin asked.

"Of course, let's go. They should be there already. But first, you must close your eyes so it will be a surprise. Grubner will lead the way."

Irvin and Hayley closed their eyes and held their hands over their faces as Grubner walked between them and grasped their elbows to guide them. As they approached the Moon Orchard, Grubner's brothers stood side-by-side admiring their work. Unfortunately, Grubner was the runt of the Trowel litter, so he could not see over them to view the cornfield.

"Open your eyes," he said as he parted the wall of siblings to take a look at his victory.

Grubner's face felt numb as his victorious smile flipped upside-down. He fell to his knees and buried his face in his hands.

"I'm surprised all right," Irvin said as he scanned the carnage in the pasture. The Ravishers had returned, and the new crops were entirely lost.

"And what in the blazes, may I ask, is that?" Irvin asked as he pointed to the middle of the ravished cornfield.

"It is the scared-crow," Grubner replied. "We built it to scare the Ravishers, just like you said. After all, humans don't have Ravisher infestations."

The only thing left standing in the cornfield was a giant black crow erected atop a tall wooden pole. It had ruffled feathers and extra-large eyes, gaped open like it had seen a ghost. Grubner's creation appeared to be the only scared thing in the Moongarden today.

"I said scarecrow, S-C-A-R-E-C-R-O-W," Irvin shouted as the letters morphed from his body and bulged from his chest one by one.

"Stop teasing him," Hayley said.

Grubner buried his head in his hands again and began sobbing.

"Everything will be okay," Hayley said as she ran and knelt beside him. "You made an honest mistake. You should use this as a lesson and learn from it as Mrs. Moongarden would."

Grubner stopped weeping and glanced up at Hayley.

"Really? Mildred would do such a thing?" He asked.

"Everybody makes mistakes, even Mrs. Moongarden, and do you know what she would do in your place?"

"What?" Grubner asked as he rose to his feet.

"She would do her research. She would study everything about Ravishers and learn what makes them tick. Then she would come up with a plan."

"But how would Grubner research?"

"You would start in The Residence study. There are many books to learn from, and Wordly Pagemore would be more than happy to help."

"Grubner will do research," he said, "Grubner will learn all about his Ravisher enemies, and Grubner will make a plan."

Grubner canceled the harvest due to unforeseen circumstances. His brothers stuck around long enough to console him and help with another clean-up. Irvin left empty-handed, but he took it well as he had expected Grubner's failure and had made other arrangements just in case.

Hayley hung around for a while after Irvin's quick exit. She must have sensed Grubner's need for her approval, so she stayed and gave him a long pep talk. Tomorrow, Grubner would begin his research, as Moonshoes would do, and then the Ravishers would be in big trouble.

Chapter 7

UNDUE STRESS

After losing his second corn harvest to the troublesome Ravishers, Grubner camped out by the Moon Orchard in case he needed to deal with any further devastation quickly. But of course, the Ravishers did not return, so Grubner stayed up half the night to no avail.

The light of the morning sky rained down on the Moongarden's lush assortment of unique plant species. Grubner rubbed the sleep from his eyes as his mouth parted into a big yawn. The unmistakable sound of Mrs. Moongarden's Snapping Spruces awakened him. Loud clacking sounds of their snaps echoed in the morning air. Something threatens them, or they would not be snapping so fiercely, he thought.

He rushed down the path towards the Moongarden's entrance and turned in a different direction near the Butterfly Shrubs. He continued past Wendy the Withering Froo and took the right fork leading to the back of the clearing where the forest thickened.

The Snapping Spruces lay calm and quiet by the time Grubner arrived, but he slowly scanned the area anyway to be sure. He gazed up at the tall, colorful trees similar to their earthly counterparts with a few significant differences. The ordinarily green or blue needles were bright red and black at the base where they were attached. Each of the branches held a small bear-trap-like appendage at the end. The yellow teeth-shaped snappers would lurch forward on long necks and bite at any critters coming too close.

The quick jog through the Moongarden reminded Grubner, he would need to wrap the Trembling Nomad pen. He had put it off for too long, so he had to do it right away. Grubner's brothers would arrive soon to look after the Moon

Orchard while he went off to study as Hayley had suggested. But now, studying would have to wait, as the seedlings would be arriving any day now.

Grubner wiped a bead of sweat from his brow as he stared into the burning Firelyte Shrub and awaited his brothers' arrival. The flames flickered off twice as he stood transfixed on the hypnotic blaze, and that concerned him because the shrub's flame should never stop until it is time.

"Rose shouldn't be dropping seeds for another two years," Grubner said to himself.

The Firelyte Shrub was an import from the elemental world of Hades, and Mrs. Moongarden named this one Rose. Like all Firelyte Shrubs, Rose stayed in a perpetual state of 'on fire,' yet she

66

would never burn. The brilliant red and orange flames swayed with the slight breeze in the air and flickered off again for a few seconds. Grubner pulled out his copy of 'Moonshoes Guide to the Moongarden' and thumbed through its pages.

"Here we are," he said and read. "A Firelyte Shrub's protective flames extinguish once every five years so its seed can drop. This event is always preceded by days of flickering."

Grubner remembered he had seen the flames blink off before, but that had been several days ago. He read more.

"After dropping its seeds, the Firelyte Shrub will reignite and start the process over. Once dropped, seeds that are disturbed or touched by external sources are rendered infertile."

Grubner sighed deeply and read the next part slowly.

"Seeds rendered infertile become firelyte capsules, which when smashed, summon a firelyte demon."

Grubner gulped and scanned the footnotes.

"I am correct. Moonshoes made a note, and it says Rose last dropped her seeds three years ago. But why—"

The following sentence gave him his answer.

"When exposed to undue stress, a Firelyte Shrub will prematurely drop its seeds."

Just as Grubner suspected, the Ravishers had been doing more than eating up all the Caretaker crops. They had been somehow subjecting the other species to undue stress as well.

When Grubner's brothers arrived, he sent three of them directly to the Moon Orchard, and the other three to walk the Moongarden proper and keep an eye out for anything out of the ordinary. Grubner continued wrapping the Trembling Nomad pen when Irvin McGillicutty showed up unexpectedly.

"How are you on this fine day?" he asked as he approached.

"No Schnickyrooners and things like that," Grubner said, "well that's a first. How may I be of assistance?"

"Irvin is here to help Grubner."

"Help? Grubner needs no help. I have everything under control."

"Of course, you do," Irvin spoke slowly as his face ballooned larger and he winked one of his now giant eyes. "But just the same, Irvin is here to tell you he requires no new orders from the Moon Orchard. Market Square is hosting a human farmers market for a few days, and the Caretakers find it an occasional treat to eat human-grown produce."

Grubner breathed a quiet sigh of relief. Irvin's news was indeed the break he needed to get the upper hand on the Ravishers. Mrs. Moongarden would be back in a couple of days, so hopefully, he would have defeated the infestation by then. Not having to constantly reconfigure, replant, and protect the crops would help.

"Whatcha doing?" Irvin asked.

"The nomads are about to drop their seedlings. So, I must wrap their pen so the little ones cannot escape. Hard to find those little sprouts when they are running around loose."

"Can I give you a hand?" Irvin asked as he morphed into a giant hand with a face.

"Everything is under control," Grubner replied as hand-Irvin mouthed the words.

"Somehow, I knew you would say that. Toodles," Irvin said and then left.

Chapter 8

STAMPEDE OF THE NOMADS

Grubner had barely finished wrapping the Trembling Nomad pen when the loud clacking noise started up again. Something had disturbed the Snapping Spruces again, so he hurried down the path to catch the mischief-maker in the act. Grabner and Gribner arrived from different directions.

"I saw two of them," Grabner said. "They ran under the brush in that direction."

"Me too," Gribner said. "You must have run right by them."

"They better not be unwrapping the nomad enclosure," Grubner said as he bolted back down the path he had entered from, and his brothers followed.

They stopped at the nomad pen and walked around its perimeter, examining Grubner's work.

"Nice wrap job," Gribner said.

"Doesn't appear to be disturbed in any way," Grabner added.

All remained silent around the Trembling Nomads, but that's what disturbed him. It seemed too quiet, and then he realized why. Rose's flames no longer burned. Someone or something had extinguished her.

"Rose must have dropped her seeds," Grubner said as he rushed over to examine her.

He studied the ground around her but found only dirt, and her blue and green leafy frame that usually blazed with orange and red flames.

"Oh no," Grubner said.

"Where are Rose's seeds?" Grabner and Gribner asked in unison as they walked up from behind.

Grubner crawled around on his hands and knees, scouring the ground frantically.

"They must be here somewhere. Firelyte seeds don't just stand up and walk away."

"Something's burning," Grabner said as his nose twitched at the air.

Suddenly, a Trembling Nomad ran by with its side branches raised at the sky. Grubner jumped to his feet and turned towards the nomad pen, now on fire. The Ravishers had the enclosure surrounded, one on each side. The closest to Grubner, the leader, turned and flashed a teeth-baring grin.

It then stretched out its long shoveling arms and opened its hands to reveal two red marbles with orange and yellow swirls. The Ravisher leader glared into Grubner's eyes and winked at him.

"The Ravishers have disturbed the seeds," Gribner said.

"They are firelyte capsules now," Grubner said. "We must stop them from igniting more of them."

Another Trembling Nomad scampered by as Grubner and his brothers slowly approached the troublesome creatures.

"It's okay, be a nice little Ravisher and hand me the seeds," Grubner said in as calm a voice as he could muster.

The Ravisher backed away as two of its minions came around the pen and joined the party. One of them held a firelyte capsule.

"Come on now," Grubner said in a hushed tone as he painted a soft smile with his face. "Nice little monster, give Grubner the capsules."

But instead, the Ravisher king tossed one of its capsules to its lackey, and now all three held one of the colorful marbles. Grubner and his brothers continued their slow advance as the creatures matched their pace, backing away. Then, the lead Ravisher started solo juggling its capsule, and the others followed along, tossing them up and catching them, tossing them up and catching them.

Grubner stared the lead Ravisher right in the eyes as a sparkle jumped from one eye to the other, and the corners of its mouth slowly ascended into a giant toothy smile. Grubner's face reddened, and his blood boiled as he knew what would happen next.

"Now! Get-em boys," he yelled as he and his brothers lurched at the creatures.

But they were too late. The Ravishers had already smashed their firelyte capsules onto the hard dirt outside the nomad pen. Three small infernos engulfed the ground between the Ravishers and Trowel brothers. The flames slowly rose from the soil as they morphed into small foot-tall fire creatures. The firelytes had black facial features, with tiny beady eyes and devilish grins.

"Never seen a firelyte for real," Grabner said.

"Me neither," Gribner added.

The brothers stared at the scene in horror as the firelytes whistled and marched in unison towards the Trembling Nomad pen. The tiny fire demons each walked to a different corner where the enclosure had not already burned. They each grabbed hold of a post and hugged it like a long-lost relative. The whistling grew louder and louder as the creatures slowly melted into their respective posts. A loud popping noise interrupted the whistling as they erupted into flames with a red puff of smoke.

The firelyte infernos spread quickly around the pen, aided by Grubner's wrapping that acted like kindling on a campfire. It only took a few minutes to burn to the ground. No sooner had the enclosure burnt down than the Trembling Nomads began to tremble. Apparently, the Ravishers could induce the nomad dance as well, and now all of the Trembling Nomads were on the loose running about the Moongarden.

By the time the enclosure finished burning, the Ravishers were nowhere to be found. Grubner assembled his brothers to assign tasks and start the rebuild. Grobner, Gripner, Gropner, and Daryl would repair the nomad enclosure while Grabner, Gribner, and Grubner tracked down the dozen missing nomads as they had seen them escape firsthand.

"Okay, are there any—" Grubner's ELMO ring interrupted him. "Hello, Miss Hayley. It is such a pleasure to hear your voice."

Grubner's talk with Hayley was short and sweet. She was checking in on him because Wordly had told her he hadn't shown up for his study session.

Grubner told her what had happened but assured her he had everything under control. Hayley said she would stop by the first chance she got.

After rebuilding the Trembling Nomad enclosure, Grobner, Gripner, Gropner, and Daryl helped search for the tiny missing trees lost in the vast forest of vegetation. They had already tracked down and returned nine of the nomads to their new corral by the time Hayley showed up.

"How goes it?" she asked as she reached the pen.

"We've repaired the damages and found nine of them," Grubner said as he silently recounted the nomads in the pen. "My brothers are out gathering the rest as we speak."

No sooner had he spoken than Grobner and Gripner approached with another missing nomad.

"They should call these things 'wandering nomads,'" Grobner said.

"What happened to you two?" Hayley asked.

Scratches covered Grobner and Gripner's arms and legs, and their clothes were tattered from head to toe.

"Found this one wrapped in a wad of Creeping Tanglers," Grobner replied.

"Had to fight them off as we untangled the poor thing," Gripner said. "Sharp little barbs those tanglers have."

"We now have ten out of twelve," Grubner said.

"Make that eleven," Hayley said as she pointed at two more brothers approaching from the direction of the clearing. "And it appears they ran into trouble too."

Mud covered Gropner and Daryl from head to toe, as well as the tiny tree they carried between them.

"Found this one in the center of the moon-pond," Gropner said.

"Of course, the little tyke got stuck in the muddy end," Daryl said. "Had to wade clear out to the middle of the muck to reach him."

"And that makes eleven," Grubner said. "Only one more to go."

"We've searched all around the Moon Orchard. But unfortunately, he isn't there," Grobner said.

"And we covered everything in and around the clearing," Daryl said.

"Well, then that leaves the Skyclimber area past the foliage tunnel," Grubner said. "Let's hope Grabner and Gribner have found him."

"They haven't found him," Hayley said as she stared into the distance, and her eyes widened. "They haven't found him because he's there." Hayley raised her arm and pointed towards the Skyclimber vine that weaved its way into the clouds.

Grubner and his brothers sighed in unison as they spotted what Hayley pointed at above the wall of foliage dividing the Moongarden. About two hundred feet up the Skyclimber, firmly planted in its side, stuck the missing Trembling Nomad.

"Well, at least we've found it," Grubner said.

Chapter 9

RGB VERSUS
WORDLY

Grubner had reached his last and final straw with the Ravishers. Their leader was obviously taunting him, and now it felt personal. Today, he would start in the study as Miss Hayley had suggested. His brothers would guard the Moongarden in his absence, and he fully expected the worst. The mischievous monsters would surely get the best of his brothers as they had him. Heck with it, he thought, even if they destroy the rest of the Moon Orchard, there were no outstanding orders. Irvin had given him a more significant gift than he would ever know.

Grubner passed by Lisa, the Butterfly Shrub near the Moongarden's entrance.

He pulled out his ELMO and tapped at its screen to make a set of double doors appear out of nowhere. He'd never gotten used to the strange sight of black double-doors standing alone against a  backdrop of rolling green hills and a blue sky. He always thought they'd look better framed in flowers. Grubner tugged open one of the doors and entered the Hall of Doorways. A light beetle clung to the ceiling and lit his way as he walked down the long black corridor filled with huge edge-to-edge doorways.

He reached the front room of The Residence and stood at the entrance to the study. But instead of entering, he turned to face a small green box sitting atop a pedestal table.

"You home?" Grubner asked.

"Sure am," Gruggins said as he sprang out of the box and landed at the table's edge. "I hear things are getting dicey in the Moongarden. My offer to help still stands."

"I know Gruggins' assistance would be valuable. But this is something I must do alone, or Moonshoes will never take Grubner seriously."

"I understand, but if you need anything, say the word."

"Well, maybe there is something. Would Gruggins study with Grubner? Grubner has never studied before."

Gruggins fluttered over and landed on Grubner's shoulder, then pointed to the study's door.

"Let's hit the books."

They entered the study quietly, and Grubner stopped.

"Looks like RGB are up to no good as usual," Gruggins whispered as they watched the scene unfold.

RGB was the collective term for three pyrodevlins named Albert, Linus, and Newton. They were nearly two feet tall with tiny slits for noses, yellow catlike eyes, devilish horns, and rows of spikes that flowed down the center of their backs to the end of their forked tails. The term was fitting due to the creatures' respective red, green, and blue colors and because they always found mischief together.

Albert stood atop the main reading table with a book held over his head, looking down beneath the table. Linus squatted on a small end table with a lamp raised above his head, ready to clobber someone. And last but not least, Newton sat on top of the bookshelves holding an upside-down wastebasket.

"Where did he go?" Albert asked.

"I saw him over here," Newton said.

"No, you didn't. He was right here," Linus countered.

Grubner stood quietly with Gruggins perched on his shoulder as they witnessed the scene unfold. A bright red dot suddenly appeared on the ground at the study's center. The pinhead-sized dot slowly moved around and traced a random pattern on the floor.

"What's that?" Newton said as he pointed at the red spot.

Albert, Linus, and Newton stared at the dancing fleck, riveted as they followed it around the carpet with their eyes like three bobbleheads.

"I think it's a blaze-mite," Albert said.

"Definitely not a blaze-mite," Linus replied. "It's a fire-nit."

"Nope, you're both wrong," Newton said. "It is an inferno particle for sure."

RGB jumped from their perches onto the floor and crawled towards the tiny spec as it raced around in ever tighter circles. They inched ever so slowly like a tiger on the prowl, and then all at once . . .

"Let's get it," Newton shouted as the three pyrodevlins sprang forward headfirst with all their might. But the dot vanished, and RGB collided with one loud thud and a puff of smoke. All that remained were three small balls on the study carpet – one red, one green, and one blue.

"What's wrong boys, all balled up and nowhere to go," a voice said from the bookshelf. The soft-spoken voice sounded like a young boy.

"Bravo Wordly," Gruggins said as he clapped in applause. "You've bested RGB yet again."

Two books on one of the shelves parted enough for a small creature to squeeze through, and Wordly Pagemore appeared. He was a four-inch bookworm that resembled a caterpillar, blue and green on top, fading to yellow at the bottom. Oval red rings with yellow centers lined his sides. He wore round glasses over his big blue eyes, which made him appear intelligent. Which he was.

Wordly had fourteen back feet for walking and six front feet that carried a small laser pointer.

The three balls slowly unraveled on the floor.

"You were all wrong," Wordly said. "Not a particle, nor a mite, nor a nit."

Loud popping noises rattled the room, followed by flashes of red, green, and blue light as Albert, Linus, and Newton emerged from being balled up.

"Light Amplification by the Stimulated Emission of Radiation," Wordly said. "Or stated simply, a LASER."

"There he is," Albert said, lunging at Wordly.

"He's mine. I saw him first," Linus said.

"Let's grab him," Newton said.

"You will do no such thing," Gruggins yelled. "I've warned you before to stop messing with Wordly. Besides, he always gets the best of you three buffoons."

RGB stopped in their tracks and turned towards the door. Grubner walked to the center of the room so Gruggins could stare them in the eye.

"Do you remember what Miss Hayley said when you harassed Pepper?"

RGB's eyes grew to the size of silver dollars as they stared up at Gruggins, like puppy dogs, and nodded.

"Miss Hayley said we would be locked up," Newton replied.

"Imprisoned with firelyte capsules," Linus said.

"No!" Albert screamed, "Not firelyte capsules. We're afraid of firelytes."

The three pyrodevlins joined hands and bolted for the out-door of the study.

"Please, please, please, not firelytes," they cried out in unison as they exited.

"Well then," Gruggins said. "Let me make the introductions. Grubner, this is Wordly Pagemore."

Wordly put down the laser pointer and held his tiny hands out to shake.

"Wordly, may I introduce you to Grubner Trowel."

Chapter 10

SCHOOL'S IN SESSION

Grubner and Wordly hit it off like old chums and made small talk for several minutes before the 'grump' in grumpling came out, and Gruggins had finally had enough.

"If I could interrupt you two new besties, I do believe there is a reason for Grubner's visit."

"Indeed," Wordly said. "How may I be of help?"

"Help, Grubner needs no help."

"But Miss Hayley said you'd be along for research," Wordly said.

"Research, oh yes, Grubner wants to study. Miss Hayley told Grubner to do his research as Mrs. Moongarden would."

"How delightful," Wordly said. "Now then, what might the subject be?"

"You mean Irvin hasn't been blabbing it all over The Residence?" Gruggins said. "McGillicutty must be slipping. He missed a spot."

"Ravishers," Grubner said. "Grubner wants to study Ravishers and learn what makes them tick. Then Grubner will make a plan."

"Ravishers," Wordly repeated. His back feet tapped at the bookshelf while his front feet rubbed together, and he stared at the ceiling. "Ravishers ravishing, Ravishers ravishing," he whispered to himself as he concentrated.

Grubner glanced at Gruggins and hunched his eyebrows.

"Nothing to worry about," Gruggins said. "It's all part of Wordly's process. Miss Hayley would not steer you wrong."

"Got it," Wordly said as he snapped out of it and quickly climbed to another shelf. His little feet were like a gecko's and allowed him to walk right up the sides and undersides of the bookshelves.

"There are four primary species of Ravishers. Each elemental world is populated by its own flavor, and they are all quite different."

Wordly disappeared behind a row of books, and one of them slowly slid out from the others on the shelf. He pushed it off the bookshelf, but instead of falling to the floor, the book floated towards Grubner as it opened to a specific page and turned upright.

"You've got the bubble blob Ravishers of Atlantis, the scorchers of Hades, the clod chompers of Ceres, and the dune harvesters of Zephyr. On each of those worlds, there are tried and true methods for ridding oneself of Ravisher infestations."

Wordly dashed from shelf-to-shelf pushing books off as he explained. They floated one by one in single file to the study table, where they gently laid themselves down. Grubner's jaw dropped open, and his eyes jumped from page to page as they glided by his face.

"He's showing off," Gruggins whispered to Grubner. "Bookworms can make a book do just about anything, but now he's showboating."

"Now then," Wordly continued, "this is where we venture into the gray area. Ravishers migrated to Earth during the Great Exodus. They migrated from all four of the elemental worlds and banded together to form a community. But that occurred many millennia ago, and earthly Ravishers have evolved a lot since then.

"So, you are saying it is possible what would work on elemental Ravishers may not work on the earthly version," Gruggins said.

"Exactly. Not much information exists on earthly Ravishers. Only a footnote in Moonshoes' Guide to the Moongarden."

The mention of his heroine and mentor piqued Grubner's interest.

"Mrs. Moongarden battled Ravishers?" he asked. "But I've read her book many times and recall no reference to Ravishers."

"Because they were not called Ravishers back then," Wordly replied as he hurried to another shelf and pushed a book off. It floated in place and opened so he could read from its pages. "There is a small footnote near the end of the section on Trembling Nomads. Here it is, and I quote: '*The*

Moongarden was visited by the ravishing earth brood today, but as luck would have it, I got by with a wee bit of help.'"

"Wee bit of help," Grubner repeated. "What's that supposed to mean? How am I to defeat the Ravishers with that advice?"

Grubner's shoulders drooped as he wiped a bead of sweat from his forehead, walked to the study table, and plopped down into a chair.

"Don't give up yet," Wordly said. "There are still some things we can try."

"Like what?" Grubner asked.

"Well, many fantastic methods exist for eliminating elemental Ravishers. I would suggest some combination of those might do the trick on earth as well. They can't have evolved all of their natural elemental behaviors away."

"Sounds like a reasonable assumption," Gruggins said. "Let's get to work."

The words of encouragement from Wordly and Gruggins pepped up Grubner's somber mood.

"Grubner is ready to study," he said as he sat upright and pounded his fist on the table.

Wordly and Gruggins stood on the reading table and helped Grubner do his research. Right off the bat, they came across one item that sounded particularly promising: a special potion called Ravanisher that worked on all flavors of elemental Ravishers. But they could only obtain it from the elemental worlds, so getting their hands on some would be nearly impossible. So, they moved on and continued scouring the literature for a solid three hours. Grubner took diligent notes as Gruggins and Wordly took turns to read passages from the books Wordly had gathered. They found references to many types of traps, decoys, tricks, distractions, and barriers invented to thwart Ravishers. By the time they finished, Grubner had pages upon pages of proven methods used for Ravisher removal on the elemental worlds, and he felt pretty confident about the plan forming in his head.

"Grubner will gather helpers now," he said. "Grubner's brothers will help implement every last one of these methods. The Ravishers will surely leave the Moongarden alone once Grubner deals with them."

"And I will assemble others to help," Gruggins said, "I'm sure it won't take much talking to convince Miss Hayley to assist. But Irvin McGillicutty will be helping too, even if I have to make a few threats or call in a few favors."

"One more thing, if I may," Wordly said. "I'm

not making any promises, but I will be involved in an important meeting tomorrow. The Headmistress requires my assistance speaking with the Council of Elders, and we will be teleporting to the elemental world of Zephyr. I may be able to get my little hands on some Ravanisher potion for Grubner."

Chapter 11

THE TRAP IS SET

After his long day of studying all about Ravishers, Grubner returned to the Moongarden to see how his brothers had fared in keeping watch. He arrived back at the Moon Orchard right around twilight, and what he found did not surprise him at all. His brothers had zonked out side-by-side in a pile of bodies. They had apparently had a very trying day. Grubner scanned the destruction. The Moon Orchard appeared more like the moon's surface than a plentiful garden of vegetation. He walked along the edge of the ravished pasture and studied the area as he combed over his research notes to cement his plan. When he returned to his pile of brothers, some of them began to stir.

"There was nothing we could do," Grabner said.

"They were too fast for us," Gribner said.

"Tricky too," Gropner added, "and smart."

"No worries, Grubner has a plan."

"But you don't understand," said Daryl. "They are not even frightened by us."

"They laughed at us," Grobner said.

"Grubner has done his research and studied the Ravishers. Grubner knows what makes them tick."

"But—"

"Grubner's plan will stop them."

His brothers cleared away the remains of yet another ravished Moon Orchard and replanted it to align with his plan. This time there would be a more varied assortment of melons, berries, and fruits favored by most all Ravisher species. He designed it so lots of space remained between neighboring patches to make room for the trenches, traps, and snares they would be building.

Even with Moongrow, the new harvest would not be ready for at least sixteen hours, so Grubner and his brothers had plenty of time for a decent night's sleep before implementing his plan in the morning. Then, it would only be a matter of time before the Ravishers would unwittingly walk into the ambush he had so carefully planned.

Grubner arrived back at the Moon Orchard before dawn, and surprisingly his brothers did too as they were already there and raring to go. Like Grubner, his siblings didn't like to be made a fool of, so now they too had a score to settle with the

Ravishers. They straightened up and stood at attention as Grubner approached.

"Awaiting orders," they said in unison like a platoon of soldiers. "Nobody messes with the Trowel brothers and gets away with it."

Grubner's heart warmed. His brother's enthusiasm gave him the boost of confidence he needed.

"Grabner and Gribner, you'll be my ditch diggers," Grubner said. "I'll chalk off the placement of the trenches. Grobner and Gripner, you'll be building the Creeping Tangler snare. Gropner and Daryl, I'm sending you to Market Square to purchase hydro-pods, muck-bombs, and twister-mines. Two dozen of each should do it. We'll be placing those later today."

"How deep do we dig?" Gribner asked.

"Needs to be deep enough that their shoveling-arms can't hoist them out. I think up to your eye-level should do the trick."

"How do we build a Creeping Tangler snare?" Grobner asked.

"You'll need to harvest a couple of Mimicking Melon trees first. Gather as much bait as the two of you can carry, and simply place it next to the Creeping Tanglers without getting tangled."

The Trowel brothers followed Grubner's orders and got right to work while Grubner roamed the Moon Orchard and chalked off additional details of his plan.

Two hours later, more help arrived as promised. Gruggins perched on Miss Hayley's shoulder as she walked alongside Irvin McGillicutty.

"Schnickyrooners and things like that," Irvin said. "I always love the stinky smell of tumbling whisker pebbles in the midst of a hedge of stone bushes. It's rather akin to the frost pimple dumplings on a grumpling's toenail but much less interesting."

"I'll show you grumpling dumplings," Gruggins said.

"You two need to stop your bickering," Hayley said. "We are here to support Grubner."

"Of  course, how may we be of assistance?" Irvin asked.

"I've chalked off the locations where the scare devices will be placed," Grubner explained. "I'll need you to help Gropner and Daryl bury them along the perimeter of the fruit patches I configured for precisely this purpose."

"We've got three types," Gropner said, "hydro-pods, muck-bombs, and twister-mines." Daryl held the devices up as Gropner spoke.

"Aren't you forgetting one?" Gruggins asked. "I don't see any inferno traps."

"This group of Ravishers used firelyte capsules to torch the nomad pen," Grubner replied. "They are not frightened by fire, so I ruled those out."

"Smart thinking," Hayley said, "Grubner's research is paying off."

His face reddened as he basked in Miss Hayley's complement.

"I've strategically placed the devices according to the Ravisher behavior they might encounter. For instance, the scorchers of Hades always approach from the east, so the hydro-pods will be buried along the eastern perimeter because water scares them away."

"I must say, you really have thought this out," Irvin said. "I think Mrs. Moongarden would be proud of Grubner."

The team worked till sundown following Grubner's orders. They planted scare devices, dug hidden trenches, built traps and brush shelters, and scattered all manner of snares throughout the Moon Orchard. For the last part of his plan, they would create a tall watchtower as command and control. He had left a small patch of space at the Moon Orchard's center for precisely this purpose. With all his help, it only took the team another two hours to build the twelve-foot-tall structure that resembled a tree fort on stilts.

Hayley, Gruggins, and Irvin said their goodbyes and promised Grubner they would be checking in to see how well his plan worked. He felt proud of all he and his helpers had accomplished in such a short time. Grubner would sleep in the command tower from here on out, and his brothers would occupy the hidden brush shelters scattered evenly around the Moon Orchard's perimeter. They would communicate via their ELMO devices if the Ravishers returned or anything out of the ordinary occurred. But for now, they could only sit and wait.

Chapter 12

DEVASTATION

A full day and a half had passed since Grubner and team had set his plan in motion, but there was no sign of the Ravishers yet. The Moon Orchard's latest seeding grew as scheduled and would be at peak ripeness by day's end, so they expected another attack at any moment. Grubner's brothers were now his full-time volunteer staff and took turns walking the grounds while he scanned the Moon Orchard from above in the control tower.

"Any sign of earthly Ravishers?" A boyish voice said from nowhere in particular.

Grubner gazed around but did not see where the voice came from, so he climbed down from his perch to gain a ground-level view.

"Who said that?" Grubner pivoted in a circle to scan the area.

"Up here," Wordly Pagemore said. He stood upon a closed book hovering a few feet above Grubner's head. A small package dangled from a string a few inches below.

"Sorry, I remember you being taller," Wordly said as his book taxi floated down to Grubner's eye level.

"Not a hide nor hair of them," Grubner said as his arms folded across his chest. "I'm beginning to think they have retreated. Now that Grubner knows what makes them tick."

"Maybe, but they could also be playing you."

"Playing Grubner?"

"Remember what you learned. Ravishers are smart creatures, and the earthly version maybe even smarter."

"Smarter than Grubner?"

"Not smarter than Grubner. But in case your plan goes south, I have brought you a present."

Wordly tugged at the string tied around the book, and the package gently dropped to the soft ground.

"What is it?" Grubner asked.

"Open it," Wordly said.

Grubner knelt and tore the wrapping from the package. A small white spray bottle the size of a Coke can fell out. It had bright red writing on the side that read: Ravanisher. Grubner picked up his present and stared at the label.

"Grubner is thankful to Wordly. But Grubner needs no Ravanisher potion if there are no Ravishers to vanish."

"Of course not. Your plan is a suitable one. But all proper plans must have a fall-back in case something goes wrong. This is Grubner's backup plan."

"Yes," he agreed, "Ravanisher is a good fall-back for Grubner."

After coaxing Grubner into creating a brilliant backup plan, Wordly said his goodbyes and floated away on his book taxi. Grubner returned to his roost in the command tower and promptly contacted his brothers via ELMO. He needed to put them at ease because he now had a backup plan.

Two more days passed, and still no sign of the Ravishers. Miss Hayley, Irvin, and Gruggins had stopped by on separate occasions, and Grubner proudly proclaimed victory over the nasty critters. Miss Hayley came bearing news of her own, Mrs. Moongarden would be returning in two days. So, he would have to harvest the Moon Orchard's crops and donate them to the vendors at Market Square before her return.

Grubner and his brothers took up their usual positions as the daylight gave way to nightfall. They would guard the Moon Orchard for one more night, and the harvest would take place first thing in the morning. Grubner took one last look over the quiet untouched garden as the proud feeling of accomplishment coursed through his veins. An hour later, he and all of his brothers fell fast asleep.

The early dawn light had just peeked out from the dark when loud cries for help erupted from Grubner's ELMO and jolted him awake.

"Mayday, Mayday," a voice said.

"We are under attack," said another.

Grubner jumped to his feet and hurried to the edge of his lookout. One of his brothers ran towards him, screaming at the top of his lungs as his arms waved in the air like streamers.

"The Ravishers have returned," Gribner said, "and there are more of them."

"Keep calm," Grubner said.

"But you don't understand," Gribner replied.

"We must stick to my plan," Grubner said as an enormous ball of water slammed against the command tower and knocked him down.

"As I was about to say, they have dug up all of the scare devices and found a way to aim them."

Screams rang out from the direction of the fruit patches. Grubner wiped the water from his soaked eyes and face and returned to his feet to witness the commotion. Grabner ran through a patch of strawberries from a miniature tornado, chasing after him and weaving a path of devastation in its wake.

"Help, help. They're after me," Gropner's voice cried out from another direction as he backed

away from a group of three Ravishers. He held a long stick and poked at the creatures to fend them off as he back down a row of blueberries. Grubner watched as the Ravishers slowly advanced on his brother like lions stalking their prey. Gropner neared the end of the blueberry patch when Grubner remembered something.

"Jump the trench, jump the trench," he shouted.

But it was too late. Gropner took one last step backward and disappeared from view as the hidden ditch swallowed him up.

"Where did he go?" Grubner asked no one in particular. "Those trenches are only supposed to be eye-level deep."

Gribner climbed through a small trapdoor in the floor and joined Grubner in the command tower.

"It's the Ravishers," he said. "They dug them deeper. We found mounds of dirt out near Mimicking Melon hill."

Gribner pointed to the piles of freshly dug-up soil at the base of the knoll. Grubner rushed to the other side of the watchtower to take a look, but his eyes quickly darted to the commotion at the top of the hill.

"Is that Daryl?" Grubner asked.

"I think so," Gribner replied.

Daryl hung upside down from a Mimicking Melon tree, and his arms gyrated in a circular motion like a baby bird trying to fly.

Suddenly, the command post shook like thunder as a giant glob of mud plastered its side. It was a direct hit, and more than the tower could handle.

"I'm feeling dizzy," Gribner said.

Grubner's eyes widened as they met Gribner's, and they both realized the watchtower was slowly falling sideways, and they were about to crash. Grubner barely had time to react and latched onto a corner post as Gribner grabbed hold of him. The tower slammed into the ground and crumbled into a box of ruins, knocking them both unconscious.

The Ravisher onslaught raged on for another hour before Grubner and Gribner awoke. They were groggy but quickly regained their composure.

"Our brothers need our help," Grubner said.

"I'm with you," Gribner replied.

"You cut Daryl down while I pull Gropner from the trench," Grubner said.

"Sounds like a plan."

"We'll meet near the south side of the strawberry field to search for Grabner. It's the last place I saw him."

Grubner and Gribner split up to help their brothers and returned to the strawberry patch within fifteen minutes. Between the four of them, it only took another five minutes to find Grabner's kicking feet sticking out of the ground. He had fallen face and arms first into a deep hole the Ravishers had dug to tunnel into Grubner's trenches.

"Five of us are accounted for," Grubner said. "But where are Grobner and Gripner?"

119

"Shh, do you hear something?" Gribner asked.

The brothers quieted down to listen for what Gribner heard.

"I hear it," Grubner said.

"Voices," Gropner said, "they're coming from that direction."

"The Creeping Tanglers," Grubner replied. "The voices are coming from the Creeping Tanglers."

The five brothers ran towards the sound of the garbled voices and arrived to find what Grubner had feared. A giant black ball of thorny vines with arms and legs poking out from all directions.

It took them over an hour to free their entangled siblings, and by the time they finished, they were exhausted and covered in scratches. The defeated look on his brothers' faces said it all, so Grubner sent them home. He felt ready to finally admit defeat, and it was time for the Trowel brothers to throw in the towel.

Chapter 13

A WEE BIT OF HELP

After his brothers' departure, Grubner roamed the Moon Orchard to survey the latest devastation. It quickly became apparent that the earthly Ravishers were far more intelligent than their elemental cousins. They had found and thwarted every piece of Grubner's plan. The traps sprung, the decoys exposed, and the snares used against his brothers. But what bothered him the most was that he let Mrs. Moongarden down. She left him in charge of her life's work, and he failed to handle a clan of nasty critters in her absence.

Grubner came to a small clearing of what were once rows of ripe blueberries. He glanced past the graveyard of upturned blueberry mulch, where several of the other patches stood undisturbed. A curious grin hopped onto Grubner's lips as motion in the distance grabbed his attention. The Ravishers were gathering in the strawberry patch to finish it off, and there were eight of them now. He felt a rush of warmth crawl down his face and slowly envelop his body. His jaw knotted shut as his teeth ground together and his fists clenched. Grubner neared full-on rage mode when he remembered Wordly's visit and the present he had left.

"Grubner is not defeated yet," he said to himself as he let out a deep sigh. "Grubner still has a backup plan."

He spun around on his feet and dashed for the crumbled remains of his watchtower. He made it there in no time and began sifting through the rubble. The command tower's cabin remained primarily intact but flattened by the crash. So Grubner plopped down onto his hands and knees and crawled around till he found a crevice he could squeeze into. He turned on his ELMO flashlight to light his way through the dark interior as he inched his way around, frantically searching. Within minutes he emerged from the ruins, hopped to his feet, and held up the can of Ravanisher.

He sprayed some into the air to test its range. A stream of white liquid shot out ten feet in front of him, and a giant cloud of vapor enveloped the area. Grubner held his breath but caught a tiny whiff of a chemical odor.

"The Ravishers will vanish now," he said as he bellowed out a sinister laugh.

He ran as fast as his short legs would carry him to the edge of the strawberry patch. The Ravishers continued munching down a row of strawberries. They marched side-by-side like soldiers as their long arms shoveled the crops into their mouths in unison. Grubner took in a deep breath as his sweaty hand tightened around the can of Ravanisher.

"Well, here goes nothing."

Grubner let out a wailing sigh and walked straight at the Ravishers, on a collision course with the chomping chorus line of teeth. When they got within twenty feet of one another, the Ravishers stopped and glared at him. But Grubner kept walking straight towards them as he slowly raised the can of Ravanisher.

Finally, he closed to a mere six feet from them and stopped to open fire. The stream of white foamy liquid shot out like a firehose drenching the line of Ravishers. He emptied the entire can for safe measure, and when he finished, a thick white vapor hovered over the strawberry patch.

He sat on the ground and buried his face in his clothing to wait for the cloud to dissipate.

Several minutes went by, and the Moon Orchard sat silent. Grubner opened his eyes and rose to his feet, but the Ravishers had left. He breathed a short-lived sigh of relief, but then the sound of something rustled behind him. He spun around on his feet and came face-to-face with the lead Ravisher and his seven minions. They had quietly moved behind and closer to him, and now they laughed at him with a cackling roar.

Grubner slowly backed away from the Ravishers as their hissy laughs grew louder. He had opened the gap to ten feet when the creatures began matching his speed to maintain the distance. Their laughing grew deafening and more annoying when it abruptly stopped. Movement on the ground tickled the corner of his eye, so he turned and looked down in time to see a Trembling Nomad seedling dashing between him and the line of Ravishers. Grubner instinctively stepped in front of it and bent down to scoop up the tiny sprout and protect it. But when he rose to face the Ravishers, they were gone.

On his way to return the seedling to its pen, Grubner pondered how it could have gotten loose in the first place. But he remembered that the Ravishers burned down the enclosure after he wrapped it, and he never instructed his brothers to re-wrap it during the rebuild.

He passed by Linnie the Itsy Bitzy bush. All of her dwindle-berry cones were brimming with berries and needed harvesting.

"Grubner's chores are piling up," he said as he glanced at the tiny seedling and spoke to it as Mrs. Moongarden would. "And on top of it all, now I need to track down all of you little wee bits."

Grubner stopped in his tracks as the words resonated in his head.

"She got by with a wee bit of help," he whispered as he spun around, and his eyebrow raised like a mad professor's. He looked down at the dwindle-berries as a wide grin strode across his lips. "A wee bit of help indeed."

Grubner hid out near the few patches of crop that had yet to be ravished. Hours went by, and nightfall approached when the Ravishers finally returned. They were not as orderly this time, instead choosing to hang out and eat solo like a group of teenagers.

He wasted no time and marched right past two of them as he strode to the group's center to face their leader. The minions quickly closed in and surrounded him in a tight circle. They began to cackle, but Grubner stood his ground and flashed a devilish smile back at the leader. He held a small red cone full of dwindle-berries he emptied into his free hand.

"One-two-three," Grubner said as he dropped the cone, plucked three berries from his hand, and pocketed the rest.

Undeterred, the Ravishers advanced slowly as their cackling grew louder.

"Three near-halvings oughta be wee bit enough." Grubner popped the dwindle-berries into his mouth and swallowed.

He stared back at the approaching Ravishers as they grew larger and larger. It took less than a minute for him to shrink down to size. Finally, Grubner knelt, picked up the red cone, and placed it on his head like a sorcerer's hat. The Ravishers' mouths shrank as their eyes expanded larger, and they backed away from itsy Grubner.

"Boo," Grubner said.

Swiftly, all at once, the Ravishers popped up off the ground as their long shoveling arms took over as legs. They turned away from Grubner and ran away like a herd of wild ostriches.

"A wee bit of help indeed," Grubner said with a victorious smile.

Chapter 14

THE AFTERMATH

After discovering the Ravishers' fear of tiny things, itsy Grubner took a victory stroll. He found it fun seeing all of the Moongarden's beauty from the perspective of a seedling. But he did still have a long list of chores to complete before Moonshoes return. So, he cut it short and swallowed three shrunken dwindle-berries to grow back to size.

He knew the Ravishers would be back, so he ordered one hundred 'itsy Grubner' garden gnomes to place around the Moongarden to frighten away Ravishers.

In the meantime, Grubner called his brothers back into service and gave each of them enough dwindle-berries to shrink down to wee-sized and wander the Moon Orchard. His brothers happily accepted their new task as it would be fun to scare the dickens out of the Ravishers for a change.

Grubner called Miss Hayley on his ELMO to tell her all about his victory over the pesky Ravishers. She sounded happy for Grubner and promised to spread the word to Gruggins and Wordly.

Mrs. Moongarden would be returning in one day, and the wedding would be the day after. With the Ravishers under control, it would now be simple to restore everything to normal before Moonshoes return. Irvin even stopped by to put in a new order once he caught wind of Grubner's successful Ravisher removal.

Mrs. Moongarden arrived early the following morning and was 'pleased as pickles' at the job Grubner had done. She was especially 'tickled' by Grubner's surprise, he had framed the doors to the 'Hall of Doorways' in a beautiful arrangement of flowers. But tomorrow was the ceremony, so she had a long list of chores for him to attend to in preparation.

Grubner reported to the clearing to help Rosebud iron and fit tiny wedding dresses onto Alicia's many apples. Irvin would be along shortly to deliver Percy's tuxedos, but he already pressed, fit, and numbered them to match Percy's pears. So Grubner only needed to assist with the dressing.

Rosebud, Grubner, and Irvin had nearly finished dressing Alicia and Percy for the ceremony when Mrs. Moongarden arrived.

"Oh my," she said, "Alicia is such a beauty, and Percy is as handsome as a Skyclimber."

"Everything is going as planned," Rosebud said. "And I couldn't have done it without Grubner. He's been an amazing help."

"Speaking of Grubner," Mrs. Moongarden replied. "Irvin tells me you dealt with a Ravisher infestation in my absence."

"Um, well, uhhh," he mumbled.

"I want to know," she said.

Grubner thought he was in for a scolding and did not know how to answer.

"How in the fiddles did you get rid of them?"

"A wee bit of help," Grubner said, "that, and I ate three dwindle-berries and turned into Itsy-Grubner gnome."

"Fiddlesticks, why didn't I think of that?"

"But you defeated the Ravishers," he said.

"I didn't have the dilliest of an idea what to do. If it weren't for the seedling hatch, I might never have rid myself of those nasty creatures. I got lucky, but you are resourceful and figured it out on your own."

"But—" Grubner said.

"But what?"

"Moonshoes only chose Grubner because Rosebud was too busy."

"You were always my first choice. I told you Rosebud offered to help, but Grubner was my only choice.

Grubner blushed as his teeth peeked through his gaping grin of a smile, and he straightened his posture.

"Moonshoes chose Grubner first," he said.

"Yes, but I have one last thing to ask of you."

"Name it, and Grubner will do it."

"Will you officiate Alicia and Percy's wedding?"

"But, Grubner has no proper clothing to wear," he said and drooped his head at the ground.

"Have no fear. Irvin is here. I'll hook you up with the old McGillicutty special. I am the resident seamstress I'll have you know."

Grubner perked up at Irvin's kind gesture.

"Grubner will officiate the wedding," he said.

The wedding was an hour away, and most of the guests had arrived already. It would be a quick ceremony, and the crowd would be small, but that didn't make Grubner any less nervous.

Miss Hayley approached as Grubner paced back and forth. Two of his dearest friends escorted her, Gruggins on one shoulder and Wordly on the other.

"I'm glad you will be officiating the ceremony," Hayley said with a bright smile.

"Thank you, but Grubner is very nervous."

"Nothing to worry about," Gruggins said. "If you can defeat Ravishers, you can do anything."

"Grubner got lucky," he said. "The Ravishers foiled all of Grubner's plans, even his backup plan."

"You mean the Ravanisher didn't work?" Gruggins asked.

"Of course, the Ravanisher worked," Wordly said.

"But it didn't," Grubner said.

"Yet it did just the same," Gruggins said.

"Ravanisher never existed in the first place," Wordly said. "Gruggins and I made it up. We made it up to give you something to believe in."

"To pump Grubner up with confidence," Gruggins added.

"But why would Gruggins and Wordly do such a thing?"

"They did it because they believe in you," Hayley said. "They did it so you would believe in yourself as much as they do."

"We knew if you believed in yourself, the Ravishers didn't have a chance," Gruggins said.

A tear rolled down Grubner's cheek as he understood what his friends told him.

"And if Grubner believes in himself," he said, "a wedding ceremony is nothing to be nervous about."

The guests sat quietly as angelic music filled the air. Mildred and Rosebud were seated in the front row while Miss Hayley, Gruggins, and Wordly sat behind them. Grubner's brothers took up the row behind them, and in the back, Irvin McGillicutty sat with a few other unfamiliar Caretakers.

Grubner stood at the end of the aisle, looking at the small stage nestled beneath an apple tree and a pear tree. Alicia looked stunning with each of her bright red apples dressed in tiny white wedding dresses while her leaves flitted in the light breeze. And Percy was equally as dashing with his plump pears dressed in mini-tuxedos like pudgy grooms.

Grubner quietly strode the aisle with an upright and confident stride. He took the podium and began speaking.

Grubner finished his short speech and proceeded with the ceremony. Alicia and Percy joined branches, and he proclaimed them husband and wife. Mrs. Moongarden was the first to compliment him on the wonderful job he had done, and that meant the world to Grubner.

Now he knew for sure, his hero and mentor, Mildred Moongarden held him in the highest regard. But in the process, Grubner learned something even more important – if you believe in yourself, you can accomplish anything.

THE END

Journey into the World of
ETHAN FOX BOOKS

Ethan Fox Books is an exciting new franchise brought to you by E. L. Seer. The Ethan Fox Books website can be enjoyed alongside the Ethan Fox Books *original series*. You can discover behind the scenes information from the author, learn more about your favorite characters, play games, enter contests, and much more. It is FREE to join and use and is designed to be safe for people of all ages. https://EthanFoxBooks.com.

As you mouse around our Site, there are hidden links from the Seers (the eyes on the **Ethan Fox and the Eyes of the Desert Sand** book cover that turn into chapter spoilers, teasers, secrets, and excerpts.

Communicate with your favorite characters by email any time. If you can't find an email address for a character in the Ethan Fox Book series, Bella is your go to person to contact; contact her by email at BellaWentworth@EthanFoxBooks.com.

MAYHEM IN THE MOONGARDEN Illustrated

Chapter Book debut by E. L. Seer. Seer is a prolific writer – but it was all getting to be too much content for the Ethan Fox Books *original series*. But with some coaxing and encouragement from his publisher, she felt his stories must be told. Hence, the spinoff of the Illustrated Chapter Books – side stories and back stories.

Ethan Fox and the Eyes of the Desert Sand book #1, in the Ethan Fox Books *original series* by E. L. Seer. After barely escaping abduction at the hands of Grimleaver vampires, thirteen-year-old Ethan Fox encounters a girl he is deeply drawn to. The two young strangers discover that they share a bond, both missing memories of their past. Together, Ethan and Hayley are lured away, awakening at The Residence, a mysterious parallel world within our own. There, they unravel the mysteries of their tangled pasts and help the Caretakers protect the human world from the Grimleavers and their evil plans to enslave humanity.

Wordly Pagemore's Early Worm Activities & Games book – Meet Wordly Pagemore! The newest series of the Ethan Fox Books franchise. Wordly Pagemore's Early Worm Activities & Games, book #1, is shaped around the Ethan Fox Books *original series*; book #1, Ethan Fox and the Eyes of the Desert Sand by E. L. Seer. More than 40 Ethan Fox Books character word search puzzles, 35 quiz Q&A match characters to their sayings: Who Said That? And 235 Trivia Q&A: How well do you know the story? Activities and games to play in paperback or print out for FREE online at the Ethan Fox Books website. https://www.EthanFoxBooks.com.

KidsStagram Blog – Join the conversation. Nicholas Knight keeps us up to date on news, editorials, interviews, discussions, fandom, event reports, and responds to a variety of rumors. It's your source for everything Ethan Fox Books. https://www.KidsStagram.com.

E. L. Seer is a husband-and-wife team – E for Eric and L for Lori. She writes non-fiction works and he writes fiction works. Eric writes the Ethan Fox Books *original series*, and the Ethan Fox Illustrated Chapter Books. Lori writes the Wordly Pagemore's Early Worm Activities & Games series, and the Wordly Pagemore's Educational Books and Board Games (coming soon).